Purple Ribbons

Written by Cristina Guarneri   Illustrated by Heather Castles

AuthorHouse™ UK Ltd.
500 Avebury Boulevard
Central Milton Keynes, MK9 2BE
www.authorhouse.co.uk
Phone: 08001974150

First published by AuthorHouse 7/26/2007

ISBN: 978-1-4343-1760-5 (sc)

Library of Congress Control Number: 2007904454

Printed in the United States of America
Bloomington, Indiana

This book is printed on acid-free paper.

authorHOUSE®

Purple Ribbons

Written by Cristina Guarneri   Illustrated by Heather Castles

For most of the time Bennie was taken care of by her mother, Mrs. Bunny.

Mrs. Bunny took care of Bennie's lunch for school, did all the laundry, and even made sure that the floors were always clean.

But what many didn't know was that Bennie had a GREAT dad.

He liked to play catch and read stories with her. Bennie's dad was a tall bunny and he loved to help all sorts of people. He would even teach Bennie how to bandage others when they got hurt and even how to listen for a heartbeat.

Bennie knew her dad had an important job. He was a medical soldier in the military, but what Bennie didn't like most was when her dad would have to go away on what Bennie would call trips. She always felt alone. Even her mom, Mrs. Bunny would become sad when Mr. Bunny would go away. Bennie knew it was important for her dad to leave, but she never completely understood why he would have to leave and go to other places far away.

Every day Bennie would wait for the mailman, Mr. Parsnip to come. She liked to receive letters, but on this particular day Bennie was unhappy to get the mail today. Bennie's dad was being called away and she didn't know what to do. "Maybe I'll hide his letter?," though Bennie. "No, that would only make things worse for her and for her dad, thought Bennie. Instead she sat on the front porch of her house still holding her dad's letter in her hand.

Bennie continued to hold her dad's letter. She had held it so tight that she almost ripped it. Tears were coming down her face so hard that a large puddle of water sat next to her. She didn't want her dad to go, but she knew that she would have no other choice but to tell him. So she picked herself up and went into the house to give him his letter.

Bennie walked up to the front door and into the living room where Mr. Bunny was sitting. Bennie watched as her dad sat reading the town paper. Bennie could feel herself start to tear up again, but she knew that she needed to be brave. As the tears started to fill up Bennie's eyes Mr. Bunny folded up his newspaper and asked, "What is wrong Bernadette?" "Why the long face?"

Bennie couldn't answer. She just stood
there. She tried with all her might, but
she knew she couldn't do it. She couldn't
tell her dad of his leaving. Bennie took
the letter and slowly handed it to him.

As soon as Mr. Bunny looked at the envelope he knew that they were his order to go away for a little while. Orders were what the military sent whenever Bennie's dad was being sent somewhere far away. Mr. Bunny opened the envelope and read his orders. Even though he was sad to leave Bennie and Mrs. Bunny, he knew that there were soldiers who needed him.

Bennie's tears seemed to last for days. Mrs. Bunny in the coming weeks was busy preparing her husband's uniforms for his leave the following day. Mrs. Bunny was sad inside too, but she knew Mr. Bunny would return to her. Besides she knew that she needed to be strong for Bennie. Bennie was having a hard time and she started to become angry for her dad's position in the military. "Why do so many people need him? I need him too," thought Bennie. Bennie stomped her feet back and forth as loud as she could on her bedroom floor. Mrs. Bunny knocked on Bennie's door to see if she was alright. "Bernadette, please stop making so much noise. It's time for bed. Now put on your pajamas and go to sleep. We have a busy day ahead of us," said Mrs. Bunny.

Bennie put on her pajamas, crawled into bed, kissed her teddy bear Wilbur and tried to fall asleep. Bennie didn't sleep at all during the night. She tossed and turned and even prayed that her dad would not have to go away. But as the morning sunlight entered her bedroom window she could hear the moving around of her parents as Mrs. Bunny finished the last of her husband's packing.

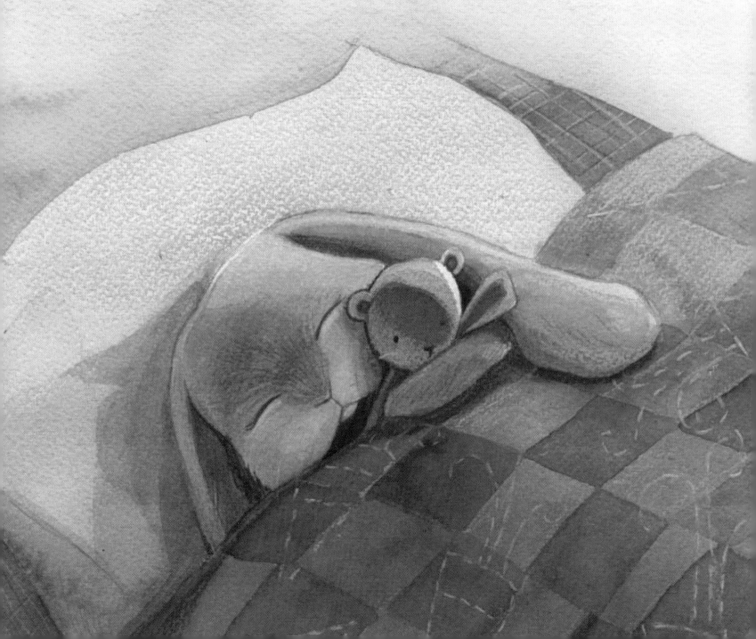

Bennie could hear the noise of her parents. Bennie got out of bed with her teddy bear. Bennie walked down each step dragging Wilbur on the floor. She met her dad at the front door just in time before he left. Mr. Bunny turned to say good-bye to Bennie and Mrs. Bunny. "It won't be long before we see each other again," said Mr. Bunny.

Bennie gave her dad a hug and watched him as he walked further and further away from home. She watched until she could not see him in her sight anymore. Bennie believed her dad when he said that he wouldn't be gone long, but she still wished that he didn't have to go.

With each passing day Bennie would send letters and pretty cards to her dad. She liked getting mail back from him. Bennie knew her dad was okay and she couldn't wait for him to come home.

She didn't understand why he had to go away when she needed him too. So in her next letter she decided she would ask him.

Dear Dad,
I miss you very much. Mommy says you will be home soon, but why must you go away when I need you here too.

Love, Bernadette
XOXO

A week later Bennie received her dad had written her back and here's what he had to say:

My Dearest Bernadette,

I know how hard it is for you and for mommy while I am away. I am helping man hurt soldiers who need lots of care. They have no fami, or friends here so I am here to help them. But I'm also here to help them heal so that can return home to their families just like me.

I will see you very soon.
Love, Dad XOXO

When Bennie read her dad's letter she felt silly for not wanting to share her dad.
Bennie now felt proud of her dad for all the things that he was doing while away.
She asked herself, "What can I do to help dad too?"

Bennie couldn't figure out what to do. She thought about sending cookies, but she always would do stuff like that. "What can I do?" thought Bennie. She knew that this would take some time to figure out and she had plenty of time to figure it all out. As the days went on Bennie's mom, Mrs. Bunny received a letter stating that Mr. Bunny was finally coming home. Bennie knew that this would be the best time to show support for her dad and that was exactly what she did. Today was the day. Bennie was very excited because her dad was coming home today. She couldn't wait for him to see her surprise.

As Mr. Bunny came up to the house, with his suitcase in hand, he was overjoyed with excitement. The house was dressed completely in purple ribbons.

"I did this for you, dad," said Bennie. Bennie ran down the front steps to her dad's arms. "I did this just for you."

Bennie's dad replied, "This is a wonderful surprise Bernadette."

"I want to be just like you," answered Bennie

"You mean by helping people?" asked Mr. Bunny.

Bennie immediately replied, "YES I DO!"

Bennie later told her dad that she knew as she got older there was nothing more that she would want to be but, just like him.

Printed in the United States
86010LV00002B